StepMonster

For Ellie, and stepmothers everywhere
J. N.
To my Granny
E. C.

EGMONT
We bring stories to life

Book Band: Gold

First published in Great Britain 2015
This Reading Ladder edition published 2016
by Egmont UK Limited
The Yellow Building, 1 Nicholas Road, London W11 4AN
Text copyright © Joanna Nadin 2015
Illustrations copyright © Eglantine Ceulemans 2015
The author and illustrator have asserted their moral rights
ISBN 978 1 4052 8221 5
www.egmont.co.uk
A CIP catalogue record for this title is available from the British Library.
Printed in Singapore
58741/2

Series consultant: Nikki Gamble

The StepMonSter

JOANNA NADIN

Illustrated by

EGLANTINE CEULEMANS

Reading Ladder

Tom was an unusual boy. One of his eyes was blue and the other was green. He had a birthmark on his bottom in the shape of a bee. And his favourite animals were moles, manatees and woodlice.

The most unusual thing about Tom
was that his mum had run away to join
the circus. So now she swung high on
the trapeze, and swallowed fire, and
walked the high wire on her tiptoes.

And her name wasn't Mrs Butterworth
any more, it was Flying Frida.

And Tom missed her, but not too much,
because his dad made the best
cheesecake in the county,

and he could
darn socks,

and trap spiders,

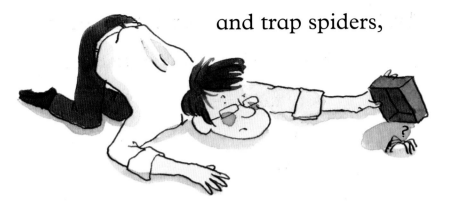

and play <u>patience</u> for seven hours
at a time.

So it was a good life, and Tom wouldn't
have changed it for all the tea in China.

But one day, it changed anyway.
Tom was fooling around with some
woodlice when his dad came in.

'I have some news,' his dad said, in a
voice that seemed to smile.

'I hope it's a pet mole,' thought Tom.
'Or a trip to the moon, or the world's
biggest marble.'

But it wasn't a mole or the moon or a marble. It wasn't even a new kind of biscuit. It was something very different indeed.

'Tom,' said Tom's dad, 'I've got a new friend I would like you to meet. She's a lady. She's lovely. And she's called Lulu.'

Tom had a think for a minute. Because he was a thoughtful boy.

'Do you like her as much as I like woodlice?' he asked.

'Almost,' said Tom's dad.

'Is she as pretty as a manatee?' asked Tom.

'And as clever as a mole with a moustache?'

'Prettier than an angel or a sunflower,' said Tom's dad. 'And cleverer than the cleverest scientist in the whole wide world.'

'Oh dear,' thought Tom, and he went as pale as a pint of milk.

Then he went green, like a bowl of pea soup.

Then he went and hid in his wardrobe, where it was dark and smelled of feet.

The trouble was, Tom knew that lovely lady friends called Lulu soon turned into stepmothers. And he knew all about stepmothers from the books he had read.

He knew that some stepmothers poisoned you with the red side of an apple. He knew that some stepmothers made you sweep the chimney and sleep in the fireplace.

And he knew that some stepmothers sent you into the deep, dark woods with your sister, never to return.

And, even if they looked pretty, they were actually rotten inside. They had slugs for tongues, and tails like newts, and a big black hole instead of a heart.

In fact, they weren't really stepmothers at all.

They were stepmonsters!

Tom's dad came up the stairs and knocked on the wardrobe.

'Why are you hiding?' he asked. 'There's cheesecake for tea.'

But Tom didn't want cheesecake for tea. In fact he didn't want anything at all, except for the world to go back to how it was. But the world doesn't often do that. Plus he needed a wee. So, in the end, Tom had to come out of the cupboard.

'Lulu is wonderful,' said Tom's dad. 'You'll see,' he added, 'when she comes to tea tomorrow.'

That night Tom lay in bed imagining what Lulu might be like. Maybe she had webbed feet like a toad, or wings like a wasp or a dragon. Maybe she could shrink down to the size of a beetle, or grow taller than a lamp post.

Or maybe she liked to eat small boys
and chew them slowly like toffee,
before she swallowed them down in one
big gulp.

Tom barely slept at all. When he woke up the next morning he felt terribly tired and horribly ill.

'You'll have to cancel Lulu,' he said to
his dad, trying hard to look upset.
But his dad had other ideas.

'Didn't I tell you?' he said. 'Lulu is kinder than the kindest nurse. So she can give you a spoonful of medicine and read you a story. You will be better before you can say "Jack Robinson". You'll see.'

At ten o'clock the doorbell rang.
'Maybe it's the postman,' hoped Tom.
'Or the milk lady. Or Mrs Briggs from
next door coming to moan about the
pigeons.'

But it wasn't the postman or the milk
lady or Mrs Briggs . . .

. . . It was Lulu.

Lulu was just as Tom's dad had
described her. She had eyes browner
than the fur on a monkey. She had hair
that looked like it had been spun from
pure gold. And she was indeed prettier
than an angel or a sunflower.

'Hmmm,' thought Tom. 'She doesn't look like a stepmonster.' But maybe that was a clever disguise.

'Hello, Tom,' she said, smiling widely. 'My name's Lulu.'

'I know your name,' said Tom, not in the least smiling. 'And I don't eat apples and I don't like woods and we don't even have a broom.'

'Well, that's just fine,' said Lulu. 'I don't like apples or woods either, and only witches need brooms. So I brought chocolate raisins and a game of cards and a stone that I found. It's shaped like a horse's head.'

'Hmmm,' thought Tom. 'She doesn't talk like a stepmonster.' But maybe that was a clever disguise.

That afternoon Tom and Lulu ate one hundred and twenty-seven chocolate raisins.

Then they played Beggar-My-Neighbour and Tom won seventeen times. Then they looked for other stones shaped like animals and found a badger, an eel and a duck-billed platypus.

'Hmmm,' thought Tom. 'She doesn't act like a stepmonster.'

But maybe that was
a clever disguise.

The next
Sunday Lulu
took Tom to
the zoo to see
a dozen moles
and a manatee
called Dave.

DAVE
the Manatee

The Sunday after that they made
a cheesecake. Lulu let Tom lick the
spoon and the bowl.

Then a hundred Sundays after that
Tom's dad and Lulu got married and
she really did become his stepmother.

'This will be it,' thought Tom. 'This is the day she will show us all she's not a lovely lady at all, but a fire-breathing, child-eating stepmonster.'

But all that happened is that she wore
a beautiful white dress, and everyone
ate cake and sang and danced until
even the moon was tired.

'Hmmm,' thought Tom as Lulu gave him a goodnight kiss. 'She really doesn't seem like a stepmonster at all. But maybe it's just a very clever disguise.'

But every day Lulu made Tom toast

for breakfast, just how he liked it. Then she played Ludo with him before school.

After school they paddled around in the river or climbed trees or fooled about with woodlice.

And every day Tom waited to find out whether she actually had anything monstrous hidden away. But every day he could only find good.

Until, after three hundred and seventy three days and seventeen hours, Tom decided that stepmonsters were only in stories after all.

That night, when Dad and Lulu came to tuck him in, Tom gave her an extra-tight hug. 'You're the prettiest and cleverest and best stepmother in the universe,' he said.

'I'm glad,' she whispered. 'Because I have a secret to tell you. You're going to have a baby brother or sister soon.' Tom went as pale as a pint of milk.

Then he went green, like a bowl of pea soup.

Then he scrunched down and hid
under his duvet. Because he had heard
all about little brothers and sisters.

They were MONSTERS!